Where's Stitch?

When You've Lost Your Best Furry Friend

Mark Gregston

Illustrated by Bill Kersey

Forefront
BOOKS

D1171601

Stitch was a lot like every other puppy.

She had lots of brothers and sisters. But she would soon go to a home of her very own.

She was chosen to be with Mamaw and
Poppa, who would care for her all her life.

Stitch liked to run and play, and people
would always ask where she was.

Macie would ask, "Where's Stitch?"

Poppa would answer, "She's out
running after the ball."

Maile would ask, "Where's Stitch?"

Mamaw would tell her, "She's swimming
in the pond with the horses."

Carter would ask, "Where's Stitch?"

Poppa would say, "She's reading a book by the fire with Mamaw."

Chase would run up and ask, "Where's Stitch?"

Mamaw would tell him, "She's out
taking a nap on the back porch."

Callie

Where's Stitch?

Mosely

Riggs

Angel

Jersey

Molly

Zeus

Ava

Colt

Brutus

Winnie

Molly

Cruz

Louie

Nash

Stitch

Mr. Rowdy

But as all dogs do, Stitch grew older and wasn't able to run as much as she used to.

One day, a friend asked, "Where's Stitch?"

Mamaw and Poppa looked at each other, then back to their friend. "She's at the veterinarian, and she doesn't feel very good," Poppa said.

It was at that time that Stitch
left Mamaw and Poppa.

Macie, Maile, Carter, and Chase all gathered
around. "Where's Stitch?" they asked.

Mamaw wiped a tear and said,
"Well, some say dogs cross a rainbow bridge.
Some say dogs go to doggie heaven.
And some say dogs go to a special place."

The animals asked Poppa, "Where's Stitch?"

Poppa cleared his throat and said, "I don't know, but she's not here anymore."

Then a smile crossed Poppa's face. "But she left us some memories we will never forget. And as long as we remember, we will always see her."

Poppa looked out across the field.
"I'll see her whenever I see someone
throwing a ball with their dog."

"I'll see her whenever I see a dog swimming in the pond."

"I'll see her whenever I see
Mamaw reading by the fire."

"I'll see her whenever I take a nap on the back porch."

Mamaw joined Poppa, and he held her close. "God gives us our pets for a short time to teach us lifelong lessons," he said.

"Stitch taught us to be kind to everyone and to always make time to play. She taught us to love the people and pets around us, just like Stitch loved us. But most importantly, Stitch taught us that those you love never really leave you."

The grandchildren all looked up at Poppa.

"Where's Stitch?" Poppa asked with a smile.

"She's right here, forever in my heart."